Words to Know Befo

box

bus

city

far

fill

home

near

there

truck

yet

www.rourkeeducationalmedia.com

Edited by Precious McKenzie
Illustrated by Ed Myer
Art Direction and Page Layout by Renee Brady

Library of Congress PCN Data

In the Big City / Anastasia Suen
ISBN 978-1-61810-169-3 (hard cover)(alk. paper)
ISBN 978-1-61810-302-4 (soft cover)
Library of Congress Control Number: 2012936771

Rourke Educational Media
Printed in the United States of America,
North Mankato, Minnesota

rourkeeducationalmedia.com

customerservice@rourkeeducationalmedia.com • PO Box 643328 Vero Beach, Florida 32964

In The Big City

By Anastasia Suen

Illustrated by Ed Myer

Fill up the box.

Fill it up, up, up.

Fill up the truck.

Fill it up, up, up.

Fill up the car.

Fill it up, up, up.

Where are we? Here we are.

Is it near? No, it's far.

Look at the bus.

SCHOOL BUS

Look at the train.

Look at the trucks.

Are we there yet? No.

Look at the boats.

Are we there yet? No.

Look at the big city.

Are we there yet?

Yes, here we are!

This is our new home.

After Reading Activities

You and the Story...

What was the elephant family doing?

What did they see on their journey?

Have you ever been to a big city?

How did you travel through the city?

Words You Know Now...

Look at the words from the list below. Which words start with the same sound?

box	home
bus	near
city	there
far	truck
fill	yet

You Could...Make a Map

- Make a map of your room. Where is your bed? Where is the door?

- Make a map of your house. Draw each room.

- Make a map of your neighborhood and write your address on it.

- How do you go to school? Make a map that shows your route. Add the address of your school to the map.

- Can you make a map of your school? Where is your class? Where is the library? Use a label to name each part.

- Add a compass rose to your maps. Which way is north? Which way is south? Where are east and west?

About the Author

Anastasia Suen has taught kindergarten to college level students. The author of over 100 books for children, she lives with her family in Plano, Texas.

Ask The Author!
www.rem4students.com

About the Illustrator

Ed Myer is a Manchester-born illustrator now living in London. After growing up in an artistic household, Ed studied ceramics at the university but always continued drawing pictures. As well as illustration, Ed likes traveling, playing computer games, and walking little Ted (his Jack Russell.)